We Want William!

The Wisest Worm in the World!

Rose Impey
Shoo Rayner

ORCHARD BOOKS

ORCHARD BOOKS
96 Leonard Street, London EC2A 4XD
Orchard Books Australia
32/45-51 Huntley Street, Alexandria, NSW 2015
First published in Great Britain in 1995
This edition published in hardback in 2002
This edition published in paperback in 2003
Text © Rose Impey 1995
Illustrations © Shoo Rayner 2002
The rights of Rose Impey to be identified as the author
and Shoo Rayner as the illustrator of this work
have been asserted by them in accordance with the
Copyright, Designs and Patents Act, 1988.
A CIP catalogue record for this book is
available from the British Library.
ISBN 1 84121 876 6 (hardback)
ISBN 1 84121 256 3 (paperback)
1 3 5 7 9 10 8 6 4 2 (hardback)
1 3 5 7 9 10 8 6 4 2 (paperback)
Printed in Hong Kong

We Want William!

William was a worm.
A very wise old worm.
The wisest worm in the world.
If worms had a problem
they couldn't work out,
they went to William.

"Wise William will know," they said.
"William will work it out."

"What William doesn't know
isn't worth knowing."
That's what worms told each other.

When a worm baby had measles

or mumps

or ate maggots,

Blurg!

their mums took them to William.

Come along!

9

When teenage worms wouldn't wash

or wouldn't work

or went all weepy,

their dads warned them,

We'll take you to William!

When the weather was too wet
or too warm,
and gangs of young worms ran wild,
older worms asked themselves,
"What would William do?"

One day William woke
to find some worms from
Wiggleton waiting to see him.
They had a terrible problem.
It was the worst story
William had ever heard.

The worms lived in the ground
under a school field;
Wiggleton Junior School field.
Sometimes, in the winter,
there were football matches
and snowball fights.

In the summer,
there were sports days
and school fêtes.
"We don't mind," said the worms.
"We're not complaining."

But once a year something
terrible happened.
It was so bad it made the
worms weep to talk about it.
"It's The World
Worm Charming Championship
we're worried about," they said.

"It happens in July.
People come to Wiggleton
from all over the world.
Hundreds of them,"
the worms told him.

17

"They come in their wellingtons,
with their wheelbarrows
and their windmills.
And their *secret weapons*."

"What sort of weapons?"
asked William.
The Wiggleton worms
lowered their voices to a whisper.
"All sorts of weapons," they said.

"Some we call 'Pokers'. They try to poke us out.

They use garden forks

and cricket stumps

and knitting needles.

They broggle about with
the ends of umbrellas.
We'd like to broggle *them*
with an umbrella
and see how they like it."

"Some we call 'Thumpers'.
They bang about above our heads

with lump hammers

and wooden spoons

and paddles.

They stamp their feet
and call it 'tap dancing'!
We'd like to tap dance
on *their* heads
and see how they like it."

23

"And some we call 'Charmers'.
They play music.

They sing songs.

They make up spells
and funny smells.
They try every trick in the book."

"And the trouble is, William,
some of them work.
Hundreds of worms wiggle-waggle
up to the surface.
The minute they put out
their heads, fingers grab them.
Whoosh!
But they still go
and the rest follow.
They're worse than lemmings!"

"What makes the humans do it?"
asked William. "What's it for?"

"For fun! For sport!
To see who can get the most,"
said the Wiggleton worms.
"Five hundred and eleven,
that's the record.

28

The fact is,
they set the worms free afterwards!
Those that survive.
But they're never the same again.
It's a terrible shame.
What's to be done, William?
That's what we want to know."

William was very old
and he was very wise,
but William had never heard
anything as bad as this before.

Over the next few weeks
all the worms in Wiggleton
heard about the campaign.

In schools young worms learned
how to recognise the enemy.
They learned what to do on
W-W-C-C Day.

Wiggleton worms joined
keep-fit classes

and body-building classes

and self-defence classes.

And every night,
deep in the dark, dark earth,
worms met in burrows,
to train in special *secret* units.
It was all hush-hush
and very (Sshh!) *secret*.

At last the big day came.
Every worm in Wiggleton was ready.
The very young worms
and the very old worms
were taken to a safe place
deep in the ground.
The other worms went
to join their groups,
ready for the battle.

REST
ROOM

NURSERY

On the school field
people were arriving
in cars and vans and buses.
They were carrying all sorts
of things with them,
all sorts of (Sshh!) *secret* weapons.

They were waiting for
the W-W-C-C to start.
Under the ground,
right under their feet,
the worms of Wiggleton
were ready too.

The whistle blew
and they were off.
The Pokers poked,
the Thumpers thumped,
and the Charmers started charming.
The Wiggleton Worms went wild.

An army of super-fit worms
worked against the Pokers.
They sawed off cricket stumps.

They nobbled knitting needles.

They grabbed hold of garden forks.

They even poked the odd 'Poker',
just to see how *he* liked it.

A band of brave worms
wearing hard hats
and carrying spades
gave the Thumpers a fright.
They soon put a stop
to their tap dancing!

And the rest of the worms
showed the Charmers
they had a few tricks of their own.

No one could believe their eyes.
They had never seen
anything like it.
The worms were escaping
as fast as they were being caught.

Everyone started falling out.
There were more accidents
and arguments
and fights
than after a football match.

Everyone went home worn out.
"Never again."
"What a wash-out."
"Too dangerous," they said.

Under the ground,
right under their feet,
the Wiggleton worms
were worn out too.
But they were happy
and victorious worms.

"We want William," they cried.
"Three cheers for William.
Hip, hip, hooray!
Hip, hip, hooray!
Hip, hip, hooray!!!"

Crack-A-Joke

How can you tell a worm's head from its tail?
Tickle it in the middle and see which end smiles!

What's round and bad-tempered?
A vicious circle!

WAITER! What's this worm doing in my soup?

Drowning, Sir.

HELP!

Mind-bogglingly funny jokes!

What's worse than
finding a worm in
an apple?
Finding half a worm!

What's long, pink and fluffy?
A worm in a pink angora jumper!

Did you know that
bookworms can eat through
five chapters a week!

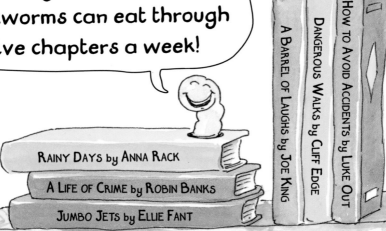

RAINY DAYS by ANNA RACK

A LIFE OF CRIME by ROBIN BANKS

JUMBO JETS by ELLIE FANT

A BARREL OF LAUGHS by JOE KING

DANGEROUS WALKS by CLIFF EDGE

HOW TO AVOID ACCIDENTS by LUKE OUT

There are 16 Colour Crackers books.
Collect them all!

❏ A Birthday for Bluebell	1 84121 860 X	£7.99
❏ A Fortune for Yo-Yo	1 84121 874 X	£7.99
❏ A Medal for Poppy	1 84121 888 X	£7.99
❏ Hot Dog Harris	1 84121 864 2	£7.99
❏ Long Live Roberto	1 84121 886 3	£7.99
❏ Open Wide, Wilbur	1 84121 884 7	£7.99
❏ Phew, Sidney!	1 84121 872 3	£7.99
❏ Pipe Down, Prudle!	1 84121 880 4	£7.99
❏ Precious Potter	1 84121 868 5	£7.99
❏ Rhode Island Roy	1 84121 878 2	£7.99
❏ Sleepy Sammy	1 84121 870 7	£7.99
❏ Stella's Staying Put	1 84121 890 1	£7.99
❏ Tiny Tim	1 84121 862 6	£7.99
❏ Too Many Babies	1 84121 866 9	£7.99
❏ We Want William!	1 84121 876 6	£7.99
❏ Welcome Home, Barney	1 84121 882 0	£7.99

1 84121 888 X

1 84121 862 6

1 84121 870 7

1 84121 878 2

1 84121 876 6

1 84121 868 5

1 84121 860 X

1 84121 874 X

1 84121 872 3